Praise for
Love at the End of the World

"Lindy Biller's *Love at the End of the World* is a revelation. Filled with the grace and grief of life, its uncanny abundance and its haunting losses, this collection of stories is empathetic, endlessly imaginative, and formally adventurous. At once precise and expansive, humorous and heartfelt, Biller's prose will leave you more attuned to the stubborn wonder and complexities of love and being alive, together and alone. As its title suggests, hope and sorrow exist as neighbors, deepened and amplified by each other. Biller's collection proves that flash fiction is both a miraculous moment and the glorious tail of a comet, lingering in your mind and in the world long after it has streaked across the page."

K-Ming Chang, author of *Bestiary*,
Gods of Want, and *Bone House*

"*Love at the End of the World* will leave you breathless and yearning for more. Lindy Biller deftly weaves these seemingly separate narratives into a tapestry of climate change and the rapture, astronauts and delivery drivers, mothers and children, gorgeous fractal patterns, circling back again and again, expanding and contracting with each wondrous story."

Melissa Llanes Brownlee, author of *Hard Skin*
and *Kahi and Lua*

"In her prize-winning debut collection, Lindy Biller writes whimsy and wonder through glittering skeletons, a crying glacier, mittens made from someone else's sweater, marigolds, monarch butterflies, a boy named Ham fighting giraffes, a pinkish-cheeked doctor. Against her memorable backdrops and characters, Biller weaves threads of religion and motherhood and life. There's dimension and identifiability in her words, an intentional surreality that softens serious subjects and makes ordinary things and people—extraordinary. Readers will be drawn to her collection's end and back again, as Biller's world and people building infuses love throughout."

Amy Barnes, author of *Mother Figures*, *Ambrotypes*, and *Child Craft*

Love
AT THE
End of the
World

stories by

Lindy Biller

Published in the United States of America by The Masters Review
www.mastersreview.com

ISBN 978-1-736-36955-5

Designed by Julianne Johnson.

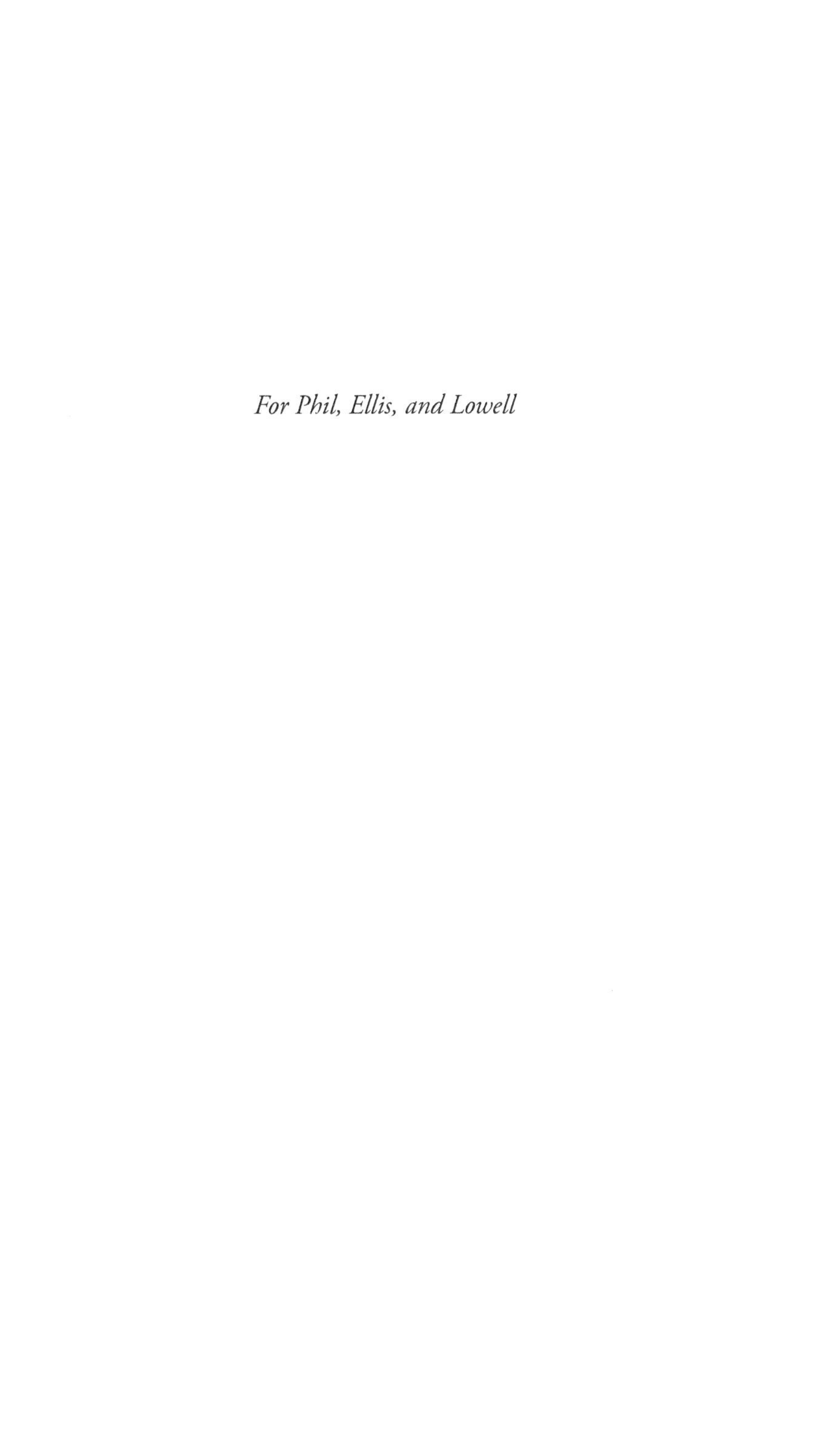

For Phil, Ellis, and Lowell

Contents

Introduction

by MATT BELL

THE FIRST THING I noticed about Lindy Biller's stories was their confidence. Story after story, Biller launches into her tales with lines evocative enough to suggesting an entire scene at once: "It's four in the morning, and the giraffes are fighting," she writes in the opening of "This Was Never Ours," one of my early favorites from this collection, and where else could I possibly want to be after that but there, finding out what happens next?

In "Extinction Event," another favorite of mine, a mother of two finds herself suddenly facing the end of the world:

By now, people were talking about it on social media, which meant the news networks would catch up in a day or two. A weather anomaly. Maybe something to do with all the wildfires. Maybe related to the vanishing, the dying pollinators. Another plague. How could it be everywhere, all at once? What did it mean?

The end of the world is a setback, to say the least, but in this case it also gives this mother a possible out from her abusive marriage—when her husband is around, we learn, "the cupboard doors were always falling off," because "he would yank them too hard, or slam them shut, or shatter her mother's china against them." We also learn that his movements are unpredictable: away as the extinction event nears, he's "due home in a few days, or maybe a week, or it could even be this afternoon."

The longer the husband stays away the better, the reader knows—and you sense the protagonist feeling it even as she won't admit it, embracing the rescue of the extinction event, which her husband might not beat home. It's a difficult, wry, and surprisingly hopeful story, and its ending was almost certainly the moment where I knew this was the chapbook to beat in this year's Masters Review Chapbook Contest.

Lindy Biller's *Love at the End of the World*, which I was thrilled to choose as this year's winner, is a book full of clear invitations and provocations, surprises and thrills. Biller's stories are frequently about motherhood and childhood and identity, about the ways our changing identities affect the way we see the world around us; Biller switches up form and voice and point of view with ease, showing off an enviable range throughout the collection. I hope you'll find her excellent stories as thrillingly bittersweet as I did. I have no doubt that they will gift you all the wonder and joy you could want, as they did me on my first read and every read since.

The Astronaut

MY SIX-YEAR-OLD WANTS to go to Mars. He dreams of floating like a dust bunny in zero gravity, looking down at the gumball sized Earth through a small, reinforced porthole. His heart, when I press my ear to his chest at night, whispers the same word over and over: *away, away, away.* I make him a cardboard box spaceship and take him to the empty lot across the street, releasing him to the December breeze. Once it would've been snowing. It used to snow all the time here. Downy pillows of white. When I was little, I rolled around in it, rolled it into round-bellied men with stone eyes and stick arms, men who shrank into glittering skeletons before collapsing. My son has never seen snow, unless you count the kind that vanishes as quickly as it falls. He wears cotton pajamas with moons and stars and rocket ships on them. He says that when he becomes an astronaut, he'll name his shuttle after me: Leili, my real name, even though he has only ever called me Mama. He rides his bike to the library and checks out books about the space program, the Big Bang theory, the entropy of stars. He launches his bottle rocket in the dirt field behind the school, speckled with broken glass and abandoned shoes and other kids' bottle rockets. My son is small for his age, and he says this will give him a better chance of survival. He will require fewer calories, less oxygen. He is thirteen before I realize how serious this is. He takes the entrance exams for the city's junior aerospace program, an Earth-to-Mars pipeline for gifted children, and he aces everything. I shut myself in the bathroom and crank on the shower and cry for twenty minutes. I go into debt to pay for his classes, his virtual books. By age sixteen he has started practical training: the flight simulator, hydroponic farming, field trips to 30,000 feet—his empty stomach heaving while the pilot flies a parabolic maneuver to simulate microgravity, my son's freefall cocooned within the curved walls of the fuselage. I start grinding my teeth at night, molars worn down to hard seeds. I buy him a telescope and help him set it up on the roof of our building. I sit out with him on clear nights, looking through the eyepiece, the long tube, the high-powered lens. My son shows me the twinkle of dead light. The pockmarked face of the moon. He adjusts the angle and shows me where I can look for him after he's gone: a luminous orange circle, smudged in places, like an old penny. I touch the hollow of my stomach and think he has always been this way: kicking, somersaulting, wide awake even at night. I'm so proud of you, I tell my son, several times a week, and he smiles, glows a little, and I imagine the words trailing after him like the tail of a comet, small pieces of me burning as he arcs upward through the atmosphere, away, away, away.

Haven

Let's say you're a thirteen-year-old girl, small for your age, a drama kid who has just discovered Shakespeare and *Rent* and *Edward Scissorhands*. You're drawn to these stories for what they don't give you: the promise of a future, the insistence that you can go anywhere, be anything. In *Macbeth*, he made his own choices, and also he was doomed from the start, because how could he have chosen any different? You want to stand arm-in-arm with your friends in a dirty, graffitied alley and sing "fuck you" to death. You dream about an airplane crashing through your bedroom ceiling, killing you instantly, and the sense of déjà vu unsettles you.

Your parents stop giving you money for drama club. We can't afford it, they say, which really means, it's a bad influence. We don't like this dark, spiky person you're becoming.

So let's say you look for a job. Just enough for club fees, costumes, fries and milkshakes at the diner. You find the perfect listing:

taking care of basement plants in an old house eight blocks from yours. The elderly couple who lives there wants to be sure they'll have fresh food, even in winter, even if the bees die out. They show you the basement. Fluorescent lights humming, metal shelves crowded with plants. You don't know the names of anything. There are fuzzy green stalks, tangled sprawling vines, orange and yellow blossoms, green teardrops tumbling from clay pots. It smells like soil and rot. You try not to breathe through your nose.

They tell you what the job would require of you: sweeping a paintbrush across the male flowers to collect pollen, dabbing it onto the stigma of the female flowers. Watering, fertilizing. The pruning of dead leaves.

There is one more person interested, the old lady says. How old are you?

Fifteen, you lie.

As you're leaving, you see a dark-haired woman coming up the front steps. She smiles at you and you wish she was your mother. Five minutes later, the old lady texts you that she's very sorry, but she has decided to go with someone else. You ride your bike home, pedaling hard, your helmet unfastened. On Johnson Street, people are stacking sandbags in front of shops and bakeries and liquor stores. There's another flash flood warning. What genius decided it was a good idea to build a city on an isthmus? (The answer is some old white men who liked the railroads and thought the lakes looked pretty.) You did a report on local flooding for school. Fifteen years ago, this area had a hundred-year flood, the kind that's supposed to happen once a century. Since then, there have been six floods like it. The city is working frantically to add more wetlands and flood walls, while conservationists beg the sandhill cranes to return. The cranes are not having it.

In an old article you dug up online, an expert listed Madison as a climate haven. The city would suffer only mild disasters: extreme flooding, heavy thunderstorms, toxic blue-green algae in the lakes. "I'd raise my kids there," he said. You think of the woman walking up the porch steps. Who the hell is she to take a job pollinating plants in a stinky old basement? Doesn't she have better things to do? Can't she leave you this one stupid, beautiful thing?

⚘⚘⚘

Now let's say you are a seventy-two-year-old third-generation Armenian woman who is still thinking about the girl who wandered through your house. Her clothes were colorful and fraying, her eye makeup smudged into bruises. You want to mother her. You'll teach her how to put her hair in a ballerina bun, instead of that messy ponytail. You'll gently discard the monstrous black scrunchie that looked like a crow perched in her hair. You'll send her home with lahmahjoon and dolma and paklava and Tupperwares full of pilaf. You'll leave out a plate of watermelon and goat cheese on the kitchen table, offer her some when she comes back upstairs, as though it has only just happened to be out. As though you eat like this every day.

Your husband looks at you carefully. "Let's see who else is interested," he says.

The next woman has brought references. Her words are low and soft, like she's speaking to a wild animal. You're not sure if she is the animal, or you are. She's a hospice nurse, looking for a side job to pay for her son's school—the Mars Project, she says, without pride or apology. Some people love the idea of training kids for a bright future somewhere far away. Others say it's nonsense, all smoke and mirrors. You offer the woman a triangle of paklava.

She thanks you, but only nibbles at the corner. She tells you her son was obsessed with trains when he was a toddler—the old, diesel-powered kind—but since then, it has been all outer space, all the time. Planets and asteroids, black holes, supernovas, red and yellow and white stars, each burning with its own loneliness. People think we could never just leave the Earth, she says. But he's been living out there his whole life.

Yes, you agree. You don't tell her about your grandmother, whose village no longer exists, whose mother died next to her in the desert, powerless to protect her. You don't tell her that Noah's Ark came to rest on Mount Ararat, the national symbol of your homeland, where the glaciers are melting. You don't tell her that the garden is for your children, who probably think you're crazy, who will put the plants out on the curb with the trash when you die. But if the worst happens, you'll be ready. You will gather them to you, your children, your children's children, and there will be fresh fruit and vegetables, sweet and fragrant herbs, a safe place for them to land. You won't say I told you so. You won't guilt them for forgetting to call on your birthday. You will keep no record of wrongs. This is what it means to be a mother.

Your husband catches your eye, proud of your restraint.

"I'm glad you'll be coming by," he says. "It gets so quiet here."

⁂

Now pretend you are a storm, gathering force over the city. You've been here before, and you'll return again soon. You've soaked deep into the natural and human-made marshes, where cranes probe for seeds and insects with needle-sharp beaks. You've poisoned ducks and fish and small dogs, leaving them scattered on the lakeshore like plastic bags and beer bottles. You have gone wherever gravity leads you, raining down, flowing south, then evaporating and migrating north for the spring. You have rinsed dirt and salt from solar-powered cars, you have formed puddles for toddlers to splash through, you have flooded basements and ditches, drowned cornfields and cherry orchards, filled rain barrels and swept humans to their death. None of this is personal. You see a girl pausing in front of a thrift store window, looking at old clothes from decades ago. You see a single mother embracing her son as he skips up the sidewalk, talking about what he learned today—how the tide is pushing the moon away from the earth, a little farther each day. You see the narrow strip of land below you, hourglass shaped, buildings jutting out of the cement like the notched bones of a fossil. You sigh and begin to fall.

This Was Never Ours

It's FOUR IN THE morning, and the giraffes are fighting.

Zara drags herself up out of her dreams, but still they cling to her, dripping slow and sticky like honey. Her husband is asleep in his hammock, snoring, one arm thrown across his eyes. She lights a lantern and goes down to the cargo hold.

The giraffes are the most fantastical creatures she's ever seen. Almost too whimsical to be real. There's something mournful in their heavy-lidded eyes, their thick lashes. She watches from the bottom step as they swing their necks against each other like heavy ropes, each thud of impact making her jump. How had the Ark ended up with two male giraffes? How had giraffes ended up here at all? Shouldn't God have seen this coming, given some kind of warning? The female giraffe sits off to the side, her long legs folded, her neck tall and still as a tree.

Elohim, Zara prayed, *Mighty One, please, please stop these things from killing each other.*

No response, of course. She has never heard God speak. Her father said it was because God doesn't talk to women. Her sons say it's because God doesn't talk to anyone, and she'd be foolish to expect otherwise. Her husband says it's because she doesn't know how to listen. Her husband, pious as a clean lamb, nothing if not obedient. But to whom?

Zara leaves the giraffes to fight and goes above deck. Beyond the railing, a dark, churning sea stretches to the horizon. The downpour has softened to a gentle rain, and she closes her eyes, letting it bathe her. She tries not to think of the screams, the unsteady lurch as the flood took up the boat on its back, the moment of transition from land to water.

When Zara opens her eyes again, her middle son, Ham, is there. She allows herself to notice how thin he's gotten. The tangled nest of dark hair, the sunken bruises of his eyes. Once he was strong and thickset, like his brothers. Has he been eating? The Ark is stocked with food: bread and honey, figs and apples, barley and other grains. But they have been careful about rationing. There is no preserved meat in the storeroom, and Ham has refused to let his father slaughter the sheep or the calves. They have come to blows over it. There is no way to know for how long the water will keep rising. Noah might have known, if he had survived. Zara and her husband can only guess.

"Sorry," her middle son says. "Couldn't sleep."

The explanation is unnecessary. Neither of them has slept in weeks. Zara is haunted by nightmares, flashes of what they have done, her guilt an apricot pit in her stomach. When she has pleasant dreams, like tonight—lost delights like baking bread, feeling the sun on her face, socializing with women like her, the existence of women like her—she always wakes too soon. But if Zara is tortured by the past, Ham is tortured by the future—the endless sea, the predators restless in their cages, the beasts of the field disoriented by their gopher-wood tomb. He cares for them day and night. His father has no interest in the animals, but he will take credit for this, too. For the ones Ham manages to keep alive. Three days ago, Ham found that the male lion had gotten loose. It was dragging one of the soft, grazing animals across the floor by its neck, leaving a dark stripe of blood. A female. One more species that no one will ever see again.

The coal-black sky has lightened to gray. From below deck, Zara hears a final thud, like a tree falling.

Soon her husband will send out the dove, the same as he does every morning. He spent a long time explaining why all of this was necessary. Ordained, even. He didn't need to explain himself to her—she was his wife, after all—but he seemed desperate for her approval. If Noah had been meant to survive, he insisted, he would have. If we weren't meant to take the Ark, God would've put a stop to it. Noah's wife had no children, couldn't have children, and that would've been it for all of us, the end of mankind, and how could Yahweh have possibly wanted that? He made us in His image. Male and female he created us. What we did was a mercy, an act of love. Drowning is said to be peaceful. I will honor him, take on his name—to Noah be all the honor and glory, and God, too, if He wants any. His words tumbling out like a stone tablet crashing down a mountain, shattered to pieces by the end. Around them, the water rising.

Now, Zara goes below deck to prepare breakfast for her husband, her sons, their dutiful wives. In the cargo hold, she sees the fallen giraffe, its breathing shallow. The victor is pacing, the nubs of its antlers grazing the ceiling. She thinks of the species they lost. The curl of its horns, the velvet of its fleece. Softer than sheep or alpaca, softer than newborn rabbits. The male has begun to refuse food. When it happened, Ham managed to entice the lion back into its cage, and then Zara helped him throw the carcass overboard before the rest of the family woke. She didn't argue with this decision, though they could've dried and salted the meat. Ham didn't refuse her help, though his mother shouldn't have been touching something so unclean. She used the rain to wash the blood from their clothes.

A hundred days from now, on a morning like any other morning, the dove will return with a twig in its beak. Zara's husband will gather the family to his breast, his wife and his sons and their wives. Zara and Ham will meet eyes while the others pray. When they land on a mountaintop lush with olive trees, her husband will fall to his knees and weep. Zara will begin to call him Noah, as he has requested, though the name curdles like sour milk on her tongue. Ham will be with them a few more years, until the curse, until his father's shame bursts forth like water from a dam. And when God hangs a rainbow in the sky, her husband will call it a sign. A miracle. *Look*, he'll say, *look at all the good we have done.*

Hivesong

THERE WAS NO chance I could be pregnant, literally none. But when the doctor said pregnancy would explain my symptoms—tender breasts, dizziness, the inability to stomach anything except water crackers and wildflower honey—I agreed to a test. What harm could it do?

My doctor had pinkish cheeks and hair like milkweed, fleecy white tufts. The softness of her face made the dislike in her eyes more piercing.

"Don't worry," she said, showing me the test results. "You have options."

She thought I was lying. The dizziness rushed back, framed floral prints swirling into the clean white walls like rainbow sprinkles into cake batter. I thought of birthdays. Hugging my mother's leg during thunderstorms. The doll I used to carry around everywhere, called Baby, who had my mother's dark hair and dimpled cheeks. Her eyes were supposed to shut when you laid her down and open when you scooped her up, but they were defective. Always half open, her pupils glossy behind a net of lashes.

"I can't be pregnant," I said. "I haven't fucked anyone in a year, at least."

The *fucked* made my doctor smile, her first real one. The *at least* kept it from being a lie. She wheeled in a fetal monitor to listen for a heartbeat.

"A false positive is possible," she said. "Rare, though."

She squirted warm gel onto my stomach and pressed the wand against my skin, searching for you. The buzzing started out faint. As she pressed harder, the sound grew—not a heartbeat, but a wild humming. The doctor frowned. "Ouch," I said, and she stopped pressing.

"The Doppler must be faulty." She tried a new machine. The humming was, if possible, louder. "It's not a baby," she said. "I'm not sure what it is."

We scheduled an ultrasound—one week away, the soonest available. On the day of my appointment, I was still dizzy and nauseous, with a new symptom—a permanent sweetness on my breath. As though my lungs had sprouted lilacs and soapwort. On the sonogram screen, the black-and-white picture morphed into a series of Rorschach tests. Clamshell, asteroid, butterfly.

Then the tech stopped moving. We stared at the screen: a honeycomb, its geometry unmistakable, a patchwork of little cells. And there you were—dozens of you, maybe hundreds, small white blurs all working tenaciously, bumping together, pulling apart.

The tech rushed from the room and returned with my doctor, who looked at the screen, then back at me. Flowers tickled my throat. Soon there were others. Another doctor, and the lady from the front desk, and two more ultrasound techs. "This is a HIPAA violation," said my doctor, the one with the milkweed hair, but no one left. No one spoke. My doctor pressed a hand to my abdomen. Not in a clinical assessment way. In the way I rest my hand on the backs of chairs to steady myself, to remember that the earth is still beneath me.

Reporters found me within days, drawn as if to the scent of clover. They called me the Bee Mom. I declined to answer their questions, hoping they would lose interest, but every day they multiplied.

"What does it feel like?"

"Do you think they'll survive?"

"What would you say to people who believe it's all a hoax?"

"What would you say to people who believe?"

My doctor was furious that word had gotten out. "This is your pregnancy," she told me. "No one else's."

"I know," I said, but I wasn't sure if I believed her. I saw the way she looked at me.

Gifts showed up on my doorstep—a twelve-pack of mason jars, a beautiful mahogany beehive frame, a beekeeper's veil. Every week, I went to the clinic and listened to you. I dreamt in hivesong. My doctor talked me through the procedure. It would need to be a C-section. My hospital room would need windows that open. I imagined the nurses in mesh bonnets and thick gloves, their excited, fearful eyes looking out. I imagined my doctor with her milkweed hair, lifting a slab of honeycomb out of me. I imagined you swirling through the room, tornado-like, and ignoring the open windows, and settling like a thick, humming blanket on my chest.

"The birth plan is only a tool," my doctor said. "As soon as it's not helping, you throw it out. The most important thing—" Her eyes filled with tears, and she couldn't continue.

I tended my garden. I read about honeybees in winter—how they form a cluster underground to stay warm. I searched everywhere for the doll from my childhood, the one with the eyes that never shut, but my mother must've thrown it away before she died.

"You're glowing," one of the photographers called out, while I was down on my knees, planting marigolds.

He was right. At the specialty grocery store, I saw her on the cover of *TIME*—the Bee Mom. Head bowed, cheeks flushed from sun. I wanted to be like her. Distant and beautiful, the way hope always is.

At home, I spread a quilt in the backyard. I tasted the honey I'd gathered—liquid gold, pale and milky, floral, fruity, acidic. I felt the first of you crawling out, a vibration on the tip of my tongue.

You Can Be Anything You Want to Be

THIS IS WHAT they tell the butterfly as she clings to a red zinnia in a fenced-in backyard, sunning her wings. That she, too, can move mountains.

The butterfly doesn't see the point in moving anything. Things are too busy moving themselves. The butterfly wants to be a freight train in her next life, roaring down a track made of dead trees and iron ribs. Full of power. Unstoppable. If a car stalls on the track, she won't be able to stop, not even if she wants to, not even if the engineer in the frontmost cavity of her skull pulls the brake and blasts the horn. People will hide behind the crooked teeth of the railroad crossing, watching in horror as she plows through the steel shell that a human left behind, crunches it like an eviction notice in her fist, leaves it mangled, continues on.

The butterfly is called a monarch. Only humans call her this, as though she is royalty, a thing to worship or to overthrow.

The butterfly has mirror wings, each reflecting the other—panes of deep orange set in symmetrical black veins. She has a proboscis like a curled-up drinking straw, but hers is biodegradable. She admires landfills, their sheer scale. Seagulls wheeling overhead looking for the shore, not finding it. Turkey vultures like satellites orbiting this new, expanding planet. If she can't become a train, she might like to be a landfill. She might like to be a human, an infant, because she too was small and squirming once, and very hungry, eating leaves and flowers and cupcakes and sausages and chocolate cake and ice cream and pickles and swiss cheese, but then she weaved herself a shroud, tasted her own death, spat herself back out. And then she felt much better.

Human babies don't have the luxury of feeling better. Mostly they feel worse. They grow, they become, they eat, eat, eat. Mostly each other. They love—sometimes each other, and sometimes other, worse things. The butterfly has been a glint of color on a botanical-themed shower curtain. A cathedral where gods come to worship. A scrap of confetti in a garden after a hard rain, dirt sprinkled over her fading wings, found by a four-year-old girl who called to her mother, wanting to show her the beautiful dead thing she has found, and the mother rushed to reassure her: it's just part of nature, it didn't feel any pain, it's just how life goes.

On second thought, the butterfly would rather not be human. They move so slowly. They bleed like fresh-picked strawberries, red and sticky, warmed with sun. The butterfly bleeds clear, like water. Once she would've flown south, following her compass needle veins, but the weather has been strange lately. The butterfly is suffering from a bad case of ennui. She flits around the trainyard like a scrap of ticker tape—the trains resting and rusted, and so lonely. She waits for them to cocoon themselves, to eat through their steel exoskeletons and grow wings. It might take some time, but she trusts their process. She listens for their heartbeat and sometimes she can hear it. It's a common misconception that butterflies don't have a heart. The butterfly's heart is a needle-thin line down the length of her body, with several matching chambers. The butterfly is sick to death of symmetry. She wants the spray-paint fungus that sprawls down the train's notched body. Giant caterpillar, endangered god, anaconda with suns for eyes. Rumbling through her black-velvet veins, as near and deep as thunder. Rolling over mountains and under them, around them and through them, but never budging them. Not an inch.

The Rapture Phenomenon

ANECDOTAL ACCOUNTS OF
SPONTANEOUS HUMAN VANISHING

Early Cases

The first known case was an influencer/weightlifter (24F) in Northern California. She had just started a live video, her movements confident and methodical as the barbell sunk low and then flung overhead, her hands white with chalk, adjusting their grip, and then her skin began to glow like the face of the moon, gleaming with the echo of sunlight—was this a new filter people didn't know about?—and then the barbell slammed to the mat where she had been standing, bouncing once, twice, then settling atop her neon-green shorts, her pink sports bra and laced-up shoes. The video kept streaming until a trainer found the phone and turned it off. Her account grew from 60,000 followers to 300,000 overnight. Paranormal investigators and social media detectives and religious fanatics combed her posts for clues. Did her ex seem abusive? Had she ever talked about flickering lights or cold spots? Was she a Christian, or was the "blessed" hashtag used ironically? Was there something about her breakfast of egg and feta toast and an acai smoothie that triggered something in her, some predisposition toward nonexistence?

❧ ❧ ❧

The second known case was a woman (47F) in rural Illinois, about forty miles outside Chicago. She had been flickering in and out of existence for decades. If any doctor had taken her complaints seriously, the phenomenon might have been studied, but the subject had a history of depression and dissociative episodes. No one noticed the flickering, except her family. Sometimes she was almost translucent. Sometimes she glowed. Her husband declined to be interviewed for this study. Her daughter reported an incident at a piano recital, another at a gas station, but said her mother didn't finally vanish until the hummingbirds started dying. The subject was driving alone to Target for a new hummingbird feeder to replace the old one, which had been destroyed by gusting winds. She veered off the road and hit a telephone pole, totaling the car, raising sparks. The power went out for three square miles. The car was found empty, with a heap of clothes in the driver's seat and a bag of Skittles spilled across the floor mat.

❧ ❧ ❧

The third, fourth, and fifth cases were scattered across the country. A natural science illustration student (46F) from Rhode Island, whose apartment was full of sketches of endangered animals that seemed like something out of a creation myth: the saiga antelope, the shoebill stork, hundreds of penny-sized jellyfish that resembled tiny ghosts. A high school science teacher (63M) in rural Maine, who disproved the hypothesis that only women were disappearing. A barista and singer/songwriter in the Twin Cities (34F) whose disappearance went unnoticed for weeks when a delivery driver moved into her split level and began taking out the trash, raking the leaves, and caring for her Bernese Mountain dog. The sixth case, of course, was the vanished toddler (2F) who finally brought nationwide attention to the phenomenon.

Complicating Factors

It is our estimation that between 0.5 and 1% of the world population has been lost, but our data is skewed by individuals who realized what was happening and simply left. Molly from Kansas City admitted that, while her husband took their daughters to ballet, she piled her clothes next to the stove, left the burner on, the kettle shrieking, and drove and drove and drove. Lauren from Kalamazoo took her family but abandoned everything else, her debt, her job in academia, her overwhelming sense of being stuck in a snow globe that someone was shaking. If the anxiety comes back, she says, they can always move again. David from Santa Fe seized on the opportunity to escape the desk job that was gumming up his arteries with cholesterol and bottomless despair. He bought a five-pound carton of Morton salt and poured it into a heap on his ergonomic desk chair. Let them think I looked back, he said.

Speaking of the Bible, our attempts to quantify the incidence of SHV have been further complicated by religious communities who refuse to report the vanishings. Their children have been kidnapped by white vans with candy. Their teenagers have been trafficked from Walmart parking lots. Their spouses have gone out to run errands and will be back any minute. This can't be the rapture, they insist, because if God is rapturing atheists and liberals and poets and babies, but hardly any Christians, what does that mean for us? In southern Ohio, New Life Church has lost only four members of their 400-person congregation: 1) the girl who always sat in the back, 2) the divorced alcoholic who used to bring the bagels and cream cheese, 3&4) two teenagers who were dating, which made people worry the vanishing could be spread through saliva or sexual contact (though there is no data to support this). The church started talking about demons. The victims glow before they vanish, and after all, doesn't Lucifer mean light? They held a prayer service (not a funeral, since their loved ones are just kidnapped or trafficked or lost in the kitchen aisle at Walmart), and my mother insisted I should come. These are people you grew up with, she said, have some compassion. It was fucking awful. A clump of people sobbing in the front row. The rest of the congregation sitting several feet back, in case non-existence is contagious. Everyone ignoring the keyboard player whose arms flickered as he switched from airy keys to church organ. The pastor staring at his hand, front and back, examining the pink flesh, the arthritic knuckles, the spidery lines where God sewed him together. Solid all the way through.

A Tired Millennial Puts on a Cardigan That Doesn't Belong to Her

I'm NOT SAYING it was fate, because fate isn't something I believe in. But I could've chosen any delivery order that day, and I chose yours—a quick drive from Jade Garden Cafe to your house, a split level with pink flowers in window boxes and a tiny yard wild with clover. You lived on the first floor, according to the online order. I knocked and rang the bell. I should've waited longer, but your taro bao was getting cold, and the ice in your milk tea was melting. I opened the door, which you had left unlocked. I poked my head inside, calling your name. And there was your yellow dress, crumpled like a snakeskin on the floor. There was the flooded kitchen sink, water gushing from the tap, streaming down the cupboards. Shiloh, whose name I learned later, bounded up to me and sniffed my sandaled feet, lingering on the fresh coat of black nail polish. He began to whine. I stroked his shaggy fur, then cranked off the water.

On the counter, your phone glowed with a notification: *Your delivery is on its way!*

I should've left. Called someone. But it was intoxicating to have small, manageable problems to solve. I tapped the *Order Received* icon on your phone. I found a towel and soaked up the water, then gave Shiloh a dog treat from the bag of gluten-free chicken bites in the cupboard. I put your iced tea in the fridge for later. Shiloh, whose name was on his collar, hadn't touched his treat. The disappearances were only rumors then, but somehow I already knew. I rubbed Shiloh's belly. I kicked off my sandals. And that was how it started.

⁂

For what it's worth, I know all of this is fantasy. You're not here anymore. You can't hear me when I pray to you. But if we had haunted this house together, instead of separately, it would've been one of those rare, beautiful things. The kind of love I've trained myself not to dream about. Every day, I scroll through your posts, your videos. I want to drink you in like spiced cider—nutmeg hair piled up on your head, freckles sprinkled like cinnamon across your cheeks. The leaves outside are just starting to change color. Your profile says that you're a queer singer-songwriter. You used to be a barista, but you're taking the summer off to focus on music. I imagine myself at one of your shows, you looking at me from across the crowded tables, eyes sparkling as you sing the song you wrote about us. The house is full of your ghosts: flipping pancakes on Sundays, humming as you water the plants, tuning your guitar, a tortoise shell pick between your teeth. We would've fought over how you always shove down the garbage when it's full, instead of taking it out to the dumpster. We would've gotten pissed at each other in line at the grocery store. We would've had tons of inside jokes, though I can't think of any. We would've slept wrapped around each other, for warmth.

ক্তক্তক্ত

The first message came from your sister, who wanted to make sure you'd heard about the wildfires. The next was one of your bandmates, asking about a show next weekend. It wasn't hard to ghost them. I'd been turning invisible for years. People tried to contact me, too—my mother, annoyed that I hadn't called her in weeks. My ex, looking for a hook-up. I turned on airplane mode. I ate the pint of crème brûlée ice cream in your freezer, then the peanut butter swirl. I made toasts for breakfast with things you had on hand—a block of feta cheese and several sweet potatoes, which I roasted with honey and olive oil. When the bread went moldy, I ordered more groceries and someone piled them on my doorstep. It hadn't rained in weeks. Sleeping in your bed felt like crossing a line, but the orange velvet sofa in the living room was perfect to curl up on. In my dream, you sang a song for me. There were two verses, a chorus, a bridge that involved screaming, but when I woke up the words vanished like smoke.

ক্তক্তক্ত

An important question: which of us would've made the coffee in the mornings? I like to think it would've been me, filling your favorite mug, you accepting it with a sleepy-eyed smile of gratitude. In your kitchen, there is a gooseneck kettle, a porcelain pour-over, light roast coffee beans, vintage mugs hanging from copper hooks, arranged in rainbow order. This is another sign that we were meant to be together. I once bought a poetry book, even though I knew it would make me cry, because the spine was sunshine yellow. Sometimes I swap the words *orange* and *green* in my head, even though the colors are nothing alike—except, I guess, that they're both colors. You would've teased me about this. You would've wondered if something happened the first time my brain encoded these words, when I was just a baby—*Green!* my mother might've said, pointing at a bush, just as it burst into flames. Yesterday, she left a voicemail to let me know that my Armenian grandparents died in their sleep. They were found by the lady who waters their plants. Mom was crying. I wish I could call her back, comfort her, but the phone is so heavy.

❧ ❧ ❧

This morning, the neighbor looked at me for a long time while I was raking the leaves. I was wearing a face mask to help filter the smoke. My hair, longer and darker than yours, was stuffed into a winter hat. Still, I think she suspects. Your family is getting frantic. Someone needs to tell them you're gone. But not now. Not yet. Yesterday I tried on one of your cardigans for the first time—the pink, chunky-knit one. It was too big. It felt soft. If you were here, you would've wrapped me in it, kissed the nape of my neck. The clouds are green today, I would've told you, pointing, and you would've held me, our bodies framed in the window, watching the sky burn.

Extinction Event

IT STARTED SLOWLY, without warnings or sirens. Astrid pulled out a box of Cheerios and found it coated in a fine layer of ash. Her fingers left circles of yellow cardboard. It was the same with everything else in the cupboard: the bear-shaped honey, boxes of cheddar crackers, bags of rice. All of it a dusty gray. She brushed off the Cheerio box and poured each of her daughters a bowl, one with milk, one without, just the way they liked it. After breakfast, she took them to the park, planted each child on a swing, googled *ash in kitchen cupboards*. Found articles about ash sapwood, ideal for building cupboards and pantries. She watched her daughters swinging. Whenever her husband was around, the cupboard doors were always falling off. He would yank them too hard, or slam them shut, or shatter her mother's china against them. The plates with the tiny orange flowers. Her husband was due home in a few days, or maybe a week, or it could even be this afternoon. His comings and goings unpredictable, like a storm. She would have to dust and wipe down everything. Still, there was no guarantee that the ash wouldn't come back.

"Push us, Mama!" the girls shouted.

She pushed them, the rusty chains groaning. Maybe it was termites? Accumulated smoke from all the charred cookies and heads of cauliflower and pot roasts she'd left cooking too long? She toyed with her wedding ring. The girls soared back and forth like birds on a string, tethered.

By evening, the ash had spread. A thin layer on the drop-leaf table, the laminate countertops. The girls giggled and drew pictures in the dust: shooting stars, princesses, dinosaurs. Astrid rinsed out a saucepan of macaroni and cheese, which came out tasting like a campfire. She called her sister in California, but the call went straight to voicemail.

It'll be okay, she imagined her sister saying, even though her sister never said things like this. She tried to think of the last thing they'd talked about, before they stopped talking. Before her husband exploded between them, his blast radius flattening everything for miles. She couldn't remember. Maybe something about winter. How cold it was here.

The next morning, Astrid made coffee, stirred Hershey's syrup into cold milk for the girls, and they sat on the porch together, watching the sun glow through a haze of ash. By now, people were talking about it on social media, which meant the news networks would catch up in a day or two. A weather anomaly. Maybe something to do with all the wildfires. Maybe related to the vanishing, the dying pollinators. Another plague. How could it be everywhere, all at once? What did it mean?

"This is not an extinction event," a scientist said emphatically.

Astrid knew denial when she heard it. She searched the

bookshelf for one of the girls' dinosaur books—bought second-hand, its pages creased and spine cracked open. While the girls played, she flipped through the full-color, sad-eyed illustrations. She read about the asteroid strike. Ash choked out the sunlight, and the world went dark, and all the plants died. Then the plant-eaters, then the meat-eaters. Except for a few, the theropods who discovered flight. Their arms became wings. Their bones lightened.

"More than 99% of the plants and animals that have ever lived on Earth are now extinct," the book said. "All major extinction events have led to a sudden burst of evolution," it added, softening the blow.

Astrid dropped off her kids with a neighbor, who was drinking margaritas and soaking her feet in a kiddie pool. "They'll be fine," she told Astrid, "go out, have some fun, you've earned it!" Astrid went to the grocery store, where panic clung to her like tar. She bought jugs of water. Toilet paper. Fruit snacks shaped like actual fruit, orange slices and strawberry and bumpy clusters of grapes. She saw church people with coal-black smudges on their foreheads, even though Ash Wednesday had been months ago. She saw a man with a curved beak like her husband's, elbowing to the front of the checkout line. She watched him slash the air open, making space for the hunger of his body.

Astrid went back home. Retrieved her daughters from the booze-soaked neighbor.

"We're going for a drive," she told them.

She packed their clothes, the dinosaur books, the matching baby dolls. She packed the last of the unbroken china. The winter gear. She packed sunscreen. She left her ring on the table, where dust immediately began to cover it. They drove.

The highway twined through the countryside, its waving

cornfields sugared with ash. It would be a four-day journey, with breaks for sleep. It didn't feel as apocalyptic as she'd expected. The rest areas were all open. The gas stations were crowded, but still operating normally. Her six-year-old read out loud about the fossil discovery on a site called Egg Mountain. Parents, eggs, juveniles. How they were covered by volcanic ash, some of the eggs unhatched. How scientists were thrilled to find a family group that had lived and died together. The girls ate snacks. They played rock, paper, scissors. They fell asleep, their bodies folded like praying hands.

Astrid turned on the radio and listened to the voices trying to make sense of things: *Scientists still have no explanation* and *People are advised to shelter in place* and *If by turning the cities of Sodom and Gomorrah to ashes he condemned them to extinction* and *Water should be strained through cheesecloth or coffee filters, then boiled before drinking.*

Astrid turned off the radio. Listened to her daughters' breathing.

I love you, she told them, until the words became only sound. A mourning dove coo.

At a playground outside Omaha, Astrid stopped to check her phone. Three breaking news updates. Thirteen texts and seven voicemails from her husband. One text from her sister: *Please, please call me.*

This time, her sister answered on the first ring.

"Astrid, thank God. Thank God. Where are you? Where are the girls?"

"Nebraska," Astrid said, and then she laughed and couldn't stop laughing. She could feel it filling her up. The lightness. Wind through hollow bones. She asked her sister to set up the spare room, and she'd call again soon. She made peanut butter sandwiches and spread a picnic blanket on the ash-choked grass.

She pushed her girls on the swing set, higher, higher, their T-shirts billowing open like wings.

Things I Know About My Mother

Her name, Leili, is of Arabic origin.

She's only one-quarter Lebanese and neither of us speak Arabic, unless you count the names of foods passed down from her grandmother—tabbouleh and fattoush and maamoul, my favorite: pale shortbread cookies dusted with powdered sugar and filled with a paste of Medjool dates. According to a quick online search, Leili means *darkness; nocturnal; night of a thousand stars.*

She's never been outside the American Midwest.

People think I'm joking when I say this, but it's true. She always wanted to travel, but things always got in the way. By *things,* I know she meant me. My father was a researcher who spent his summers in Antarctica, studying penguins. She gave me his name, in case I ever want to contact him. Only when you're ready, she said. When she talks about him, there is no malice in her voice. She loves it here. The seasons, the birds and butterflies returning each year, the spring thaw, dead things coming to life again. She has been with other people, both men and women, but none of them stuck. They come and go like the seasons, leaving flowers or ice or mild destruction—damaged gutters, fallen branches. She tells me about snow, the way it used to be, when it didn't disappear as quickly as it arrived. A blanket of quiet over everything, trees glittering with sugar. She says if you hold your breath, you can still hear the hiss as it falls.

She collects rocks and minerals.

Most of these are from the Great Lakes: pink swirled agates, yellow jasper, honeycomb coral. Petoskey stones, which seemed to be covered in reptilian eyes, unblinking. *They're coral polyps,* Mom told me once, moving my finger over the bumps. *Each eye was once a mouth.* She told me how Lake Superior formed: eruptions of magma for millions of years, then the slow cooling and hardening. The glaciers carving out a crescent-shaped scar. At night, the beach felt wild and alien, no city lights for miles. While the waves kissed my mother's feet, I looked up at the moon. Its rocky face, its cratered cheeks. *Think of how small we are,* Mom said, and yes. I was.

She has worked several jobs.

Her highest-paying job was as a nurse at a hospice center, but her favorite was as a pollinator. An old couple down the street was trying to keep a garden in their basement—an end-of-the-world contingency. *They're preppers, but the sweet kind,* my mom said. Once she brought home a winter squash and we sliced it in half, drizzled it with olive oil, stuffed it with farro and dried figs. Once, when I was fourteen, she called from the neighbor's house. "I'll be home late," she said. "Don't worry." Minutes later,

I saw an ambulance roar past, lights flashing. I ran outside in my socks, panicked, convinced she was dead. Instead, I found her talking to the paramedics as they wheeled two bodies out. She didn't see me watching. She could've been light years away.

She's seen a lot of people die.

Her work stories used to make me sad, until I learned more about the universe. How black holes fling subatomic particles into space, how we can only detect them as bursts of light, deep in the Antarctic ice. How Saturn's rings look solid, even through a high-powered telescope. The worst thing she's ever done is heroic measures on a ninety-year-old Full Code patient, rib bones cracking like peanut brittle under her hands. *Don't trust the movies,* she told me. Nothing can restart a stopped heart. A defibrillator can sense chaotic rhythms, shock them back to normal, but it can't fix what's already gone.

She doesn't want me to go.

Sometimes she cries in the shower, thinking I can't hear her. Sometimes we laugh until tears baptize our faces. Sometimes she tells me she's proud of me, and I store away her words with everything else I want to keep, even after it stops being useful: how to shape the dough for maamoul, the precise angle of my landing trajectory, the beach where we skipped flat gray stones over the water, the likelihood of being incinerated on takeoff, the tug of a rip current and how to free yourself—swimming parallel to the shore, instead of toward it.

She doesn't want me to stay.

Mom put the pollination money in an envelope marked *School.* I added the pennies and nickels I found with my metal detector.

We never touched the envelope, even when the fridge only had a head of wilted lettuce and half a block of cheese. We ate cheese on stale crackers, cutting around the moldy parts. Sometimes she drizzled honey on top, but not too much. There were hummingbirds dropping like tennis balls in people's yards. There were rumors of a woman who birthed a swarm of honeybees, which shows you how weird things had gotten. At the botanical gardens, a corpse flower was blooming, its ten-foot spadix pointing straight up into the sky like an obelisk, or a rocket. *Only once every seven years!* the sign said cheerfully. It felt like a threat. In seven years, where would we be? Visitors came from all over. Mom and me, too. We breathed the smell of rotting flesh. We watched the deep-purple frill peel itself open one last time, then slowly start to close.

Love at the End of the World

OUR WHOLE TEAM watches the launch together—a live video on my tablet—while Caleb hands out silverware and Sylvia ladles potato soup into enamel bowls. There are seven million people watching with us. I twist the ring on my finger, take it off, slide it back on again. My colleagues are worried about the seals—clumps of ash stuck to their whiskers, coating their fur, like dirty snow. The babies aren't swimming. They flop on the ice, lethargic, while their mothers float in cracks in the sea ice, calling out, urging the babies to take their first plunge.

Sylvia puts a bowl of soup in front of me. *Forty seconds to lift off.* "You okay, kiddo?"

I'm forty-nine years old, nobody's kiddo, but she's ten years older than me, her face creased with crow's feet and laugh lines, her silver hair cut short. She's the only one I've told. No, I tell her, not really, but somehow it comes out as *Fine.* She leans over my shoulder, placing a hand on my lower back. The rest of our team is chattering, slurping soup from their bowls. Space travel hasn't been awe-inspiring since the moon launch, decades before I was born. It hasn't been noble since rich men started having pissing contests about whose rocket was biggest. But Mars is worth celebrating, surely. In the comments:

The Earth is flat. Wake up.

RED PLANET, HERE WE COME!

What a waste… most expensive PR stunt ever.

I turn up the hiss of static, wondering if I might hear my son's voice again. But the status checks are done. Sylvia squeezes my shoulder as the countdown starts. Down from ten, like in the movies. Smoke gushes out to one side of the rocket—is that normal, a plume billowing like ocean waves, like a volcano spitting ash, has something gone wrong?—and then a flicker of liquid orange fire, the rocket rising, rising, a male voice saying something like, *Here we go, folks, the first manned mission to Mars,* although half of the crew are women, although this isn't the first attempt at a Mars mission, only the first one that has actually launched, and within seconds the rocket has shrunk to the size of a soda bottle, leaving a trail of fire and smoke through the steel-gray sky. Then the smoke is gone, too.

I look around the table. My team is unmoved.

"I don't know why they're bothering with Mars," Penny says, spooning broth to her lips. "I'm sure it just wants to be left alone."

❧ ❧ ❧

The email showed up in my inbox last week. There was no greeting—he must not have known whether to call me Timothy, or Professor Bell, or Dad.

You don't know me, but you met my mom 25 years ago in

Madison, Wisconsin. It's okay, you don't owe me anything, that's not what this is about. I'm leaving with Mars Alpha next Friday and I wanted you to know. Sorry this is so out of the blue. I've read some of your research on Weddell seals, and it's fascinating. Did you know that the first explorers to spend winter in Antarctica went mad? I mean, that's what they called it then. Now we'd call it psychosis. They must've felt like they'd reached the end of the world, all that ice and darkness. Like another planet. Do you ever winter over? Have you always worked with seals? Anyway, thanks for reading this, and feel free to email me if you want to. If you don't want to, that's okay, too. I'll be back in three years, if all goes well.

I showed Sylvia, and she whistled. "Damn. Your kid's an astronaut!"

Sylvia never wanted children. My wife and I don't, either. Earth is overpopulated. We have enough problems to solve, without adding more. I made an excuse and retreated to my bunk. I read the email again and again, until I knew it by heart. Until I could recite every word, lips barely moving, like a prayer.

❦ ❦ ❦

I haven't always worked with seals. Twenty-five years ago, it was Adélie penguins. My research team went to Madison to help with an outreach project—a VR game where players got to become penguins. They shifted their weight from side to side to waddle, swung their hands to fend off predators. We advised the game designers and gave an open lecture about our work. During mating season, the male penguin presents a female with a pebble. If she accepts it, they mate for life. The mother lays two eggs, and the parents take turns warming them. They protect the chicks when they hatch. It's a hard job, and most of the babies don't make it. In 2017, there was too much sea ice, and 18,000 chicks starved. In 2022, only half of the expected penguins returned to the nesting site, and no one knows why. The penguins' natural predators are the skua—predatory seabirds who eat Adélie chicks and eggs. The skua are a well-oiled machine, when it comes to killing. One skua swoops and flaps and dives in the parent's face, closer, louder, until finally the penguin waddles forward to slap the bird away. This gives another skua a chance to dart in from behind and snatch up one of the chicks. Sometimes both of them. It's over within seconds. Part of our research was examining how the penguins reacted. If both chicks were killed, did the parents stay at their empty nest, or did they return to the sea? Did they try to mate again? Did they appear to mourn?

࿇ ࿇ ࿇

After the lecture, we divided into groups for discussion. Nobody seemed to care much about the penguins. People wanted to know about life at the South Pole. Where did we sleep? Was there running water? Indoor plumbing? An undergraduate geology major asked if we ever got emotionally attached to the chicks. If we rooted for them to survive. If we ever helped them. I told her what I felt like I was supposed to say—that, obviously, humans tend to anthropomorphize, but in the end, we were researchers. We maintained emotional distance from our subjects. We let the chicks fend for themselves, no matter how cute they were.

She saw through my bullshit, but she was kind about it. I guess the skua have to eat, too, she said, shrugging.

She lived off-campus, in a redbrick building built in the 1930s, with original crown molding, a wood-burning fireplace that she wasn't allowed to burn wood in, and an enormous claw-foot tub. I thought about her for years afterward. We did everything right. There was no way anything should've happened. My gut reaction, after the email, was desolation, despair, a sense that something tiny and precious had been snatched away from me, but I knew immediately what an asshole that made me. As bad as the fucking skua.

❧ ❧ ❧

Sylvia knows that I'm in an open marriage. My wife treats my absences like I'm a whaler out at sea, except that she's not waiting around, pining for my return. Except we're not here hunting or killing or being pulled down into the deep. We're— what, exactly? It used to be easier to explain. Now, most of the funding goes to urgent projects: seed vaults, gene editing, de-extinction. When I write a grant, I have to really wax poet- ic. There is a case to be made for wonder. For research that has no immediate practical application. If the mother seal denies her pup milk until it plunges into the water, is that pup more likely to survive? How do seals learn to hunt? Is it a learned skill, or something innate? Sylvia is leaving before winter, back to Portland, and she won't be returning. I'm not sure if any of us will. While Caleb stacks the dishes—his turn today, mine tomorrow—I type up another email. Hit send. I've considered emailing Leili, too, but she might not want to hear from me, on the same day her child left the planet. She might say our son takes after me, as though it's some sort of compliment. She might say he's nothing like me at all.

❧ ❧ ❧

When I step outside after dinner, the rocket still slicing like a knife through my chest, I see blood on the ice. One of the mother seals has given birth while we were eating. The pup is whining and twisting, searching for its mother's nipple. *It's right there*, I want to tell it. *Right there, you're so close!* But the mother is too spent to move, and the baby is squirming in the wrong direction. Its eyes dark and wide, gleaming like deep wells.

The truth is, the babies are unbearably cute, and it's impossible not to get attached. I need to document the birth, tag the pup so we can track it throughout its lifespan. Instead, I watch, holding my breath. I imagine scooping the seal into my arms, feeling the weight of its warm, soft body, carrying it the last few inches.

Choose Your Own Ending

The Apex Predator

You have eaten venison and veal from deer you killed yourself. You bagged your own Thanksgiving turkey, and goddamn,
was it beautiful. Plump and colorful, with a lush rainbow of
feathers. You'll share whatever you kill with your neighbors,
but only if they have something to trade in return. You'll shoot
anyone who tries to mess with you. You aren't violent, only
pragmatic. In nature, the strong eat the weak. We've been outside of nature for so long that we've forgotten. How is hunting
less ethical than going to a grocery store and picking out slabs
of raw, bloody meat that somebody else killed? You know how
to fish, too. If all the fish die here, or if the toxic water makes
them dangerous to eat, you can follow the river north. If the
lake freezes, you'll drill a hole through the ice. You'll sit with
your pole and wait for the small, satisfying tug. If anything,
this post-apocalyptic existence will be better than what you're

used to. More streamlined. Kill, eat, sleep, repeat. You're almost looking forward to it.

The Homesteader

We have never been outside of nature. Nature is all around us, as soon as we step out the door. Even inside. Mice, spiders, the potted plants in the kitchen, the beetle crawling along your windowsill. We've already been living in ways that will help us to survive, to make meaning. We kept urban chickens, rewilded our backyards, paid thousands of dollars to have other people install wood stoves in our living rooms. When everything collapses, we will bake bread and let its warmth fill the house. We will forage with the seasons—ramps, ostrich ferns, and nettles in spring, wild berries, puffball mushrooms, and saskatoon in summer, wintergreen, black walnuts, and taproots in fall. In winter, we'll bring the chickens inside and gather around the woodstove and pull out the old furs that our ancestors handed down, or the quilts in blush pink and gray and mustard yellow that we stitched ourselves. We'll tell stories of the old world and the new one.

The Nomad

A quiet, bleak, romantic existence. Think *The Road*, but without the cannibals. You move from place to place, never stopping. You dream of a place where things are better—maybe the coast, or the CDC headquarters, or that cabin where your grandparents used to take you fishing every summer. Maybe it's Chicago, people trading canned goods and bullets on the Magnificent Mile, Lake Michigan swelling over the flood walls, skyscrapers looming like prehistoric skeletons in museums, with plenty of space to curl up in their skulls and chest cavities. As long as you have a goal, you're still alive. As long as you keep moving, you won't have to stop.

The Colonist

You are too smart or rich or beautiful to go down with the ship. You've heard about the Mars mission and it seems like the burst of excitement you'll want in your older years. In ten, twenty years, they'll probably have figured out terraforming. Maybe even an artificial atmosphere. There will be biomes for each Earth habitat you leave behind. De-extinction. Orchards and cornfields patchworking the planet. With strict guidelines, of course, to make sure that what happened to Earth doesn't happen here. You'll board your lifeboat and watch the blue planet shrink to the size of a robin's egg in your window. You won't mourn, because nothing will be lost. This is the next stage of evolution. It is a second chance. There's something poetic about the red of the Martian soil—like rust, like blood, like hunger. Soon you'll grow to love it.

Footnote

A WOMAN IN SEATTLE, who laid her sleeping toddler (2F) in the crib, kissed her soft hair, and went to take a shower. The woman felt, after this two-year trial period, that she wasn't meant to be a mother. She wished she could go back in time, try again. The daycare teachers said her daughter was gifted. She could count to twenty. She could fit shapes into their holes—triangles, squares, diamonds and hearts and crescent moons. They said, you must read to her, and the mother wasn't sure if it was a compliment or a command. She cranked on the hot water and stood under it and tried to remember a time when she'd felt human. It might've hurt less, she told us in an interview, if there had been some sort of warning of what was about to be lost. Her husband worked until midnight. When he got home, he would kiss her, as usual, then go straight to bed. He was never fully himself until morning, when he made the coffee, got their daughter dressed and changed, tossed her in the air while she giggled—once, twice, three times, always rising, always coming back down again. The woman wishes she could have a second chance with her husband, too, but there is no stopping the slow, glacial drift between them. That night, she toweled off her hair, watched three episodes of a trashy show on Netflix, ate a few squares of a chocolate bar and then the rest of the squares. She microwaved a cloth pouch stuffed with dry, uncooked rice, bought from a local craft fair, and used it to warm her feet, which were always cold. In olden days, before furnaces and forced air, they used hot water bottles for a similar purpose. Now, she sleeps with the rice pack tucked against her stomach, hugging it with both arms. If she heats it for exactly fifty-eight seconds, it feels like her daughter when she was a newborn—small and compact, radiating heat. She holds it close until the warmth fades, then microwaves it again, until she falls asleep or the sun rises.

Warm Milk

IN MY DREAM, I am making a scavenger hunt for my son, who is ten and too big for scavenger hunts. He has been too big for scavenger hunts since he was poppyseed sized, rooting around in my uterus for good soil. He always seemed so hungry—in real life, not in the dream.

You're losing weight, said my doctor, bemused, at my twelve-week appointment. *What have you been eating?* she said. I began to name the things I had fed my baby so far:

- Peanut butter
- Funfetti cake
- Hummus and pita chips
- Plums and other stone fruits
- Whole boxes of graham crackers
- Live mice
- Small terrestrial planets

Okay, the doctor said, *okay, that's good, keep doing that.*

In my dream, I fold a piece of paper into sixteenths and draw something new on each square. A pigeon feather, a baby in a stroller, a glacier, a walnut. My son and I go outside, where the asteroid hangs in the same place we left it—glowing orange in the window of sky between our maple tree and our neighbor's black walnut tree, slowly burning through the remaining lace-work of atmosphere. Scientists expect the asteroid to hit us within the week, or the month, or maybe in another fifty million years. Eventually it will get sick of hovering, watching, waiting. It will remember how to move forward. Or rather, down.

We won't find a glacier, my son says. He steps over an earthworm that has stranded itself in the middle of the sidewalk after last night's rain. *Glaciers are too good at hiding,* he says. *You can't find them if they don't want to be found.* He picks up the worm and eats it.

You're right, I agree. *We'll have to look carefully.*

I notice he's brought his mittens, the ones I made from tiny sweaters. The sweaters weren't his. I don't know whose sweaters they were. I found them in a trash bag behind our building. At first they were normal-sized, but each time I touched one it shrank and shrank. The embroidery so delicate, so impossibly tiny. I cut the sweaters apart and stitched them back together in new, hand-shaped configurations. They were in the trash, I told myself, it's no big deal, even though I knew another mother would be coming back for the sweaters, would be upset not to find them, would search and search.

But in the dream my son is here, he's holding my hand, like he used to when he was ten in real life and his friends weren't around. It seems safer not to think about the mittens or where they came from. I don't regret making them. If we meet a glacier, I'll have my skin to crawl into, and my son will have the mittens to warm his hands. They won't fit him much longer, the way he's been growing. He mows entire lawns with his teeth and the neighbors pay him extra. They are fascinated by the way he can unhinge his jaw. His father was a snake, I try to explain, an anaconda, but no one believes me except my doctor, who insists he'll grow into it.

Mom, are you even listening? my son asks.

I tell him no, and he looks so relieved it hurts. We begin to scavenge in earnest. We get down in the dirt like prehistoric humans, or kids under the age of four, or foxes in winter. Here, the walnut. There, a whole pigeons' worth of dappled gray feathers (*extra points,* my son says excitedly), and there, a dead dog, which follows us, wagging its tail, until I stop to rub its matted white fur. The asteroid will kill us soon, but still, I'd like to have a dog like this. (*Why?* my sister says bluntly, like she always does, as though I invited her, as though this dream is hers. *Why would you want a dog, why would you want another child, just for it to burn or free or starve or turn to dust?* It's a valid question, and one that I answer like a ten-year-old, or like a mother, or like any other wild thing: *Because.*)

My son is the one who spots the glacier, blending in with a white minivan.

I guess you were right, he says, head bowed against the lash of snow, feet slipping over compressed ice. My feet slip too, but we keep walking. Here is the acorn, cracked open by small hands. Here is the stroller, stuffed full of blankets and canned goods. There, on a green hill, is a whole field of bright, budding children, and people like me (like us) are wondering up and down the rows. The air smells like warm milk, the middle-of-the-night kind with nutmeg and honey stirred in. The asteroid seemslower, though I'm probably imagining it.

My son notices the look on my face. *Do you want to get inside?* he offers, and peels back his jaw like the lid of a soup can.

No, I tell him. *I'm sorry. No.*

The plants, I mean the children, have wide crimson petals and concentric circles of sharp teeth and humming crowns made of honeybees, which in my dream haven't gone extinct yet. The children are all so hungry. I want to stop and feed them, but my son grabs my arm.

We need to keep moving, he tells me.

I believe him. And also I'm not so sure. The glacier is crying. She is looking at the asteroid. She is saying she's never seen anything like it, she's saying it's the most beautiful thing in the world.

Acknowledgements

Thank you to these incredible publications, where the following stories were first published, sometimes in slightly altered forms:

"The Astronaut" in *Cheap Pop*

"Hivesong" in *Nurture Literary*

"Extinction Event" in *Flyover Country*

"Warm Milk" in *The Lumiere Review*

Lindy Biller is a writer based in Wisconsin. Her work has been selected as the winner of the 2021 Fractured Literary Flash Fiction Contest and nominated for Best Small Fictions, Best of the Net, and The Pushcart Prize. Her stories can be found in *The Masters Review*, *Chestnut Review*, *SmokeLong Quarterly*, *Cheap Pop*, *Longleaf Review*, and *Necessary Fiction*, among others. Find her online at lindybiller.com.

www.ingramcontent.com/pod-product-compliance
Lightning Source LLC
Chambersburg PA
CBHW061224210726
48294CB00006B/1973